Doyle

Yang the Youngest and His Terrible Ear

LENSEY NAMIOKA

ILLUSTRATED BY

KEES DE KIEFTE

Little, Brown and Company
Boston   New York   Toronto   London

To Father and Eldest Sister

Text copyright © 1992 by Lensey Namioka
Illustrations copyright © 1992 by Kees de Kiefte

First Edition

The characters and events portrayed in this book are fictitious. Any similarity to real persons, living or dead, is coincidental and not intended by the author.

Library of Congress Cataloging-in-Publication Data

Namioka, Lensey.
    Yang the youngest and his terrible ear / Lensey Namioka;
illustrated by Kees de Kiefte. — 1st ed.
        p.   cm.
    Summary: Recently arrived in Seattle from China, musically
untalented Yingtao is faced with giving a violin performance to
attract new students for his father when he would rather be working
on friendships and playing baseball.
    ISBN 0-316-59701-5
    [1. Chinese Americans — Fiction.   2. Moving, Household — Fiction.
3. Violin — Fiction.   4. Identity — Fiction.]   I. Kiefte, Kees de,
ill.   II. Title.
PZ7.N1426Yan   1992   91-30345
[Fic] — dc20

10   9   8   7

MV NY

Published simultaneously in Canada
by Little, Brown & Company (Canada) Limited

Printed in the United States of America

Yang the Youngest and His Terrible Ear

1

Yang the Eldest drew his bow across his violin strings, and a shower of sparkling notes fell over the room.

Yang the Second Eldest drew her bow across her viola strings, and a rainbow of notes hung brightly in the air.

Yang the Third Eldest drew her bow across her cello strings, and a wave of deep, mellow notes washed over us.

Yang the Youngest — that's me — drew my bow across my violin strings, and it went *SCREECH*.

I'm the youngest child in our Yang family of four children. According to our Chinese custom, I'm not allowed to call my elder brother and my two sisters by their given names. Instead, I have to address them as Eldest Brother, Second

3

Sister, and Third Sister. They call me Fourth
Brother.

My parents are both musicians. Father was a
violinist in the Shanghai Philharmonic Orchestra

4

until a few months ago, when we left China and came to live in America. Now he has a job with the Seattle Symphony Orchestra.

Mother is a pianist; she used to accompany

Father when he gave concerts. But she hasn't been able to find a job since coming to America. Orchestras can use many violinists, but they don't need more than one pianist. So these days Mother spends most of her time shopping and cooking to feed all of us.

It isn't easy to feed a family of six on Father's salary. He is what's called an alternate, which means he gets to play only when one of the other violinists is absent.

Father also makes some money giving private lessons. At first he didn't get many students. Parents didn't want to bring their children to a music teacher who spoke so little English and had such a strong Chinese accent.

But music is music in any language, and Father doesn't have to say much during the lessons. When one of his students plays well, he smiles. And when a student plays a sour note, Father just puts on a look of great suffering.

I know that look: when Father gives me my music lesson, it never leaves his face. I started playing the violin when I was five, and now, four years later, Father's expression is still the same.

I don't exactly enjoy the lessons, either, but I don't suffer as much as he does. That's because

6

I can't hear what I'm doing wrong. In fact that's my problem: I have a *terrible* ear.

My parents didn't believe that could happen to one of their children. They both had good ears, and so did Eldest Brother, Second Sister, and Third Sister.

Eldest Brother was humming tunes even before he could talk. Mother taught him both Chinese and American songs. Soon he was singing "Old McDonald Had a Farm," right on pitch, even on the "oink oink" and the "quack quack" parts.

On Eldest Brother's fourth birthday, my parents gave him a violin that was one-eighth the size of a regular one. He is fifteen now, and he has been right on pitch ever since.

Second Sister, two years younger than Eldest Brother, started singing along during his violin lessons. So she got a viola, one-eighth size.

Third Sister, who is three years younger than Second Sister, started by playing the viola that had become too small for Second Sister. But she was so short that she had to stand up and hold the instrument on its end, like a cello. She got a real cello as soon as she grew tall enough.

When I was born my parents were pleased, because now they could have a complete string quartet: two violins, a viola, and a cello. They never imagined that the second violin would turn out to be so bad.

But *I* knew. I began to suspect something was wrong, because whenever I started singing, people would move away from me. I loved songs — at least I loved the words. In China, we often sang American songs, and the most popular one was "Oh Susanna." But *my* favorite song was the one about the farmer and his animals, which Eldest Brother had taught me.

"Fourth Brother is singing 'Old McDonald Had a Farm,'" Third Sister announced proudly one day.

"No, he's not!" said Father. "The tune he's singing is quite different."

"Well, at least he's doing the oinks and the quacks," she said.

Third Sister has always been closest to me. It's not just that we're close in age (she's only a year older than I am), but when everyone else thought I wasn't really trying hard enough to play in tune, she was the only one who knew that I was doing the best I could.

The trouble is that except for the oinks and the quacks, "Old McDonald Had a Farm"

8

sounds to me a lot like "Mary Had a Little Lamb." I am what they call "tone-deaf."

You'd think that being Chinese and tone-deaf could be a real problem, because the Chinese language is full of tones. If you make the same sounds, but with different tones, you change the meaning completely.

Luckily, things aren't that bad for me, because the tones in Chinese slide up and down, and I *can* hear the difference between a sound sliding up and a sound sliding down. My problem is that I don't know *how much* to slide up or down. This is not good when you have to play the violin.

At least I didn't have to worry about rhythm. Having a terrible ear means I have a problem with pitch. But I can count as well as any of the Yangs, and I always come in on time. The others probably wished I wouldn't come in on time. Sometimes I suspected they wished I wouldn't come in at all.

So there I was, coming in on time, sliding up and down, doing the best I could. And as usual, my best wasn't good enough.

Eldest Brother rolled his eyes. "You have to *listen* harder, Fourth Brother!"

"Before you play, sing the notes in your head first," ordered Second Sister.

That's easy for her to say. I couldn't even sing the notes in my throat.

"Maybe he's a mutant," said Third Sister.

"A mutant?" asked Second Sister. "Don't you mean a mute? He certainly needs an extra-size mute."

A *mute* is a little button-like thing you put on your violin when you want to sound softer. Second Sister had once suggested permanent mutes on my violin.

Third Sister giggled. She's the giggler of the family because she knows her dimples are cute.

We all have our own ways of learning English, and Third Sister's is to make a list of five new words every day and memorize them. *Mutant* was on her list today.

"*Mutant* means you turn out really different from your parents," she explained. "Fourth Brother isn't lazy; he was just born different. There's nothing he can do about it."

"Nonsense," said Second Sister. She was thirteen and a young lady. Young ladies didn't giggle and didn't put up with nonsense.

"Let's stop talking and get back to practicing," said Eldest Brother. As the eldest of the

10

family, he was more serious than the rest of us. Whenever we started to waste time, he quickly got us back to work.

We immediately picked up our instruments again. We weren't scared of Eldest Brother — not very much, anyway — but we knew we had to practice.

A very important recital was being planned. For Father's sake, for the sake of the Yang family, we had to make a good impression.

At a recital, all the students play a piece of music, and their families and friends are invited to hear them. This was the first recital Father had organized since he started giving music lessons here in Seattle. If his students did well, their parents would tell other parents. Then Father would get a lot more students.

"At the end," announced Father, "the four of you will be playing a portion from a string quartet. It will be the grand finale of the whole recital."

We all knew the last piece on the program was the most important one. That was the one the audience would remember best when they went home. If we could impress the audience with our skill, we would really show them what a great teacher Father was.

Normally, I didn't suffer much during my lessons. I just ran through the piece as best as I could, and if other people suffered, too bad for them.

But this recital worried me. When they heard me playing so badly, the parents in the audience would say to themselves, "If Mr. Yang can't even teach his own son to play, how can he teach our children?"

Now as we practiced, I found myself sweating with nervousness. My hand felt unsteady, and I couldn't get a good grip on the violin bow. It slid around on the string, and produced those terrible screeches. This got on everybody's nerves.

Even Eldest Brother finally lost his patience. "It's bad enough that you play out of tune! Do you have to keep screeching, too?"

"I'm sorry," I mumbled. I wiped my hands on my pants, then wiped my brow, which was streaming. This made my hands wet again, and I had to borrow Third Sister's handkerchief.

Eldest Brother sighed deeply and put his violin under his chin. "Let's try those last four bars again."

Second Sister picked up her bow, and Third Sister bent over her cello.

12

One by one, the other three Yangs started playing their sparkling notes. When my entrance came, I pressed harder, to keep my bowing hand from wobbling. But all I got was an extra loud *SCREECH*.

A look of deep suffering came over Eldest Brother's face. At times like these, he looks a lot like Father. He has the same long face, and the same wide mouth that curves down at the corners when he is in pain.

"Fourth Brother," he said, fixing me with his sternest look, "I know that music doesn't mean as much to you as it does to the rest of us. But you really have to try harder. You know the saying, that hard work can overcome ten thousand problems."

"He just doesn't *care* about playing in tune," said Second Sister. "I don't think there's any use practicing until his attitude is better."

She put her instrument back in its case, firmly closed the lid, and snapped the catch.

I tried not to show it, but I was hurt. I admired Eldest Brother and Second Sister deeply for being so dedicated to music, even if I couldn't share their dedication. It must be wonderful to know exactly what you wanted to do. I didn't know what I wanted to do. All I knew was that

13

I didn't want to be a miserable second violin.

After Eldest Brother and Second Sister had left, Third Sister came over and put her arms around me. "Don't feel so bad," she said softly. "I know you're doing your best."

Her kindness only made me feel like crying. "I'll spoil everything. I'll ruin the recital."

"Maybe we can think of something," she said. "Maybe we can fix it so that Eldest Brother plays most of your notes."

"The only way to save the recital is for Eldest Brother to play *all* of my notes," I muttered.

In a string quartet, the second violin — me — usually has the least important part. But even playing the least important part, I could still ruin things. And Eldest Brother couldn't always cover for me. He had his own notes to play.

There was no way, absolutely no way, that I could play in the recital without sounding awful. And if I sounded awful, the whole quartet was going to sound awful. And since our quartet was the last piece, the audience would go home with an awful impression of the recital.

I wanted so much to please my family, but it seemed hopeless. Maybe Third Sister was right:

I was a mutant. I would never be one of the musical Yangs.

What if I got so sick that I couldn't play? When the others saw me in pain, they'd feel sorry for criticizing me. I'd be lying, pale and suffering, in bed, and I wouldn't be around for them to pick on anymore.

But maybe they wouldn't be sorry. I was no good. My parents might even be glad if they could exchange me for someone else. Someone with a good musical ear.

Then I realized that I was wallowing in self-pity, and I became disgusted with myself.

I remembered Father's anxious face as he counted heads when we boarded the plane coming to America. I remembered his big smile when he saw all four of us safely strapped in our seats. I remembered Mother carefully dividing a Hershey chocolate bar with almonds into four exactly equal pieces. My parents did love me as much as the others, I knew that.

But what could I do to prevent the recital from being a disaster? I had managed to get out of tight spots before. When I was singing in the chorus of my Chinese school, I always looked around at the person behind me whenever the music teacher scowled in my direction. But this wasn't so simple.

I had to think of something to save the recital. I just had to.

2

Our family arrived in America in the winter, and the school year was almost half over. So when I started school, the other students in my class already knew each other. To make things worse, I didn't even know enough English to try to make friends.

But language was only one of my problems. American kids scared me at first. They yelled terribly loud and ran fast in the hallways.

For the first few weeks, I found myself hugging the walls. It was like the time in China when I learned to swim. I was afraid to let go of the side of the pool because in the middle were other swimmers splashing around like sharks.

Once when I was walking in the hallway at school, I turned a corner and bumped into a boy.

17

He was running so fast that he knocked me off my feet.

He pulled me upright and shook me a little. Maybe he wanted to see if any parts were rattling loose. When he saw that I wasn't hurt, he winked at me, laughed, and said, "Hey, no sweat!"

He looked so cheerful that I laughed, too. "No sweat" sounded like a good phrase, and I told Third Sister about it. She added it to her list.

In a few weeks I learned to walk just as fast and shove my way just as hard as the other kids.

My parents even complained about it. "You're becoming too rough, Yingtao. Why do you have to stomp your feet so hard?"

Before I got used to the American school, the other kids laughed at some of the things I did. Each morning, as soon as the teacher came into the room, I jumped to my feet and stood stiffly at attention. That was how we showed our respect to the teacher in China.

The first time I did it here, the teacher asked me whether I needed something. I looked around and saw that nobody else was standing up. Feeling foolish, I shook my head and sat down.

When I did it again the next day, a couple of kids behind me started to snigger. After that, I remembered not to jump up, but I half rose a few times. One boy used to watch me, and if he saw my bottom leave my seat, he would whisper, "Down, Fido!"

Third Sister was a great help during those early days. While the other kids were busy talking or playing games at recess, she and I stood in a corner and kept each other company.

Every day we walked together to our elementary school, which was not far from our house. Eldest Brother and Second Sister took a big yellow bus to a school that was farther away.

If Eldest Brother had trouble making friends, it didn't seem to bother him. Music was the only thing he really cared about.

I think Second Sister felt the loneliest. In China, people always said she would turn out to be a real beauty. She had been popular at school there, always surrounded by friends. But in America not many people told her she was beautiful. These days she was often cranky and sad. Mother told the rest of us that we just had to be patient with Second Sister.

Third Sister had no trouble at all making

friends. Even before she could speak much English, she began chatting with other kids. She could always fill in the gaps with laughter.

During lunch she and I sat at a table with mostly Asian-Americans. At first we didn't understand what Asian-Americans were. When we were filling out registration forms at school, we put down "Chinese" in the space marked "race."

The secretary at the school told us to change it to "Asian-American." With a big smile, she said, "We have a number of Asian-Americans at this school, so you'll be able to make friends easily."

My teacher must have felt the same because on my first day in class, she seated me next to a girl who was also Asian-American.

I greeted her in Chinese, but she just shook her head. "I'm afraid I don't understand Japanese," she said in English.

"I wasn't speaking Japanese," I told her. "I was speaking Chinese."

"Sorry. I don't understand that, either. My family is from Korea."

I didn't know much about Korea, except that my country had once invaded her country. I hoped she didn't hold it against me.

"You speak good English," I said. "When did you arrive?"

"I was born in America," she said. "So were my parents."

In spite of this bad start, she tried to be helpful to me. But we never became close friends.

So I was lonely. After Third Sister made friends in her class, she began to spend less and less time with me.

Then I met Matthew. During recess one day, Third Sister was busy talking to some new friends, and I was looking wistfully at some boys playing catch and wondering if I could find the nerve to join them.

Suddenly I felt someone pluck my pen from my pocket. This was a ballpoint pen I had brought with me from China, with a picture of a panda on the side of it. Whenever I thought about China and missed the friends I had left behind, I would take out the pen and look at the picture.

The boy who had taken the pen was running away, laughing. I ran after him, shouting. The teacher came up and asked me what the trouble was.

"He took my . . . my . . . " I stopped, because I didn't know the English word for pen. In Chinese we have the same word, *bi*, for pen, pencil, and brush. "He took my writing stick," I finished lamely.

The boy who'd taken the pen stood there and grinned, while the teacher looked puzzled.

"Jake took his ballpoint pen," said a tall, freckled boy with curly brown hair. "I saw the whole thing."

The teacher turned and frowned at Jake. "Is this true?"

"Aw, I was just teasing him a little," said Jake, quickly handing the pen back to me. "He's always playing with it, so I got curious."

I thanked the boy with the curly hair. "Don't mind Jake," he said. "He didn't mean anything."

"My name is Yang Yingtao," I introduced myself. Then I remembered that in America people said their family name last and their given name first.

"Yingtao is my last name," I told him. "Except that in America my last name is really my first name and my first name is my last name. So I'm Yang Yingtao in China and Yingtao Yang in America."

The boy looked confused. Just then the bell

22

rang. "I'm Matthew Conner," he said quickly. "See you around!"

I began to feel a little less lonely.

We discovered that our school had an after-school orchestra, which met twice a week. My parents thought that Third Sister and I were very lucky, and they signed us up for the orchestra right away. They never even asked us whether we wanted to join.

Before Third Sister and I could play in the orchestra, the conductor gave us an audition; that is, he asked each of us to play a few bars of music alone.

He looked pleased when he heard Third Sister play the cello. He immediately put her near the front of the orchestra.

Then it was my turn to play the violin. He stopped me after only four measures and looked at me thoughtfully. "Would you like to try the triangle instead?"

Maybe I should have felt insulted, but in fact I was tempted to accept. You don't need a good ear to play the triangle, since all you do is just hit it with a stick. You only need to come in on time, and I was good at that. And besides, the triangle makes only a small tinkle, so you can't do much harm.

But I knew my parents would be upset. "I have my own violin," I told the conductor unhappily. "My parents will expect me to play it."

He sighed. "Very well. I know what parents are like." He put me in the very last row of the violin section — as far away from the audience as possible.

When I took my place, the boy sharing a music stand with me said, "Hi, looks like I'll be your stand partner."

It was Matthew, the boy who had gotten my pen back. I was very glad to see him.

Then the conductor raised his stick and the orchestra began to play.

When playing together with other people, my trick was to draw my bow back and forth, without quite touching the strings. This helped everybody. It helped me; it helped the other players; it helped the conductor; and most of all, it helped the audience.

After a few bars we stopped playing while the conductor tried to cheer up the trombone player, who was making bubbling sounds when he tried to blow.

Matthew turned to me. "You don't play very loudly, do you? I couldn't hear you at all."

"You're lucky," I told him.

He looked puzzled, but I had no time to explain because the conductor raised his stick again.

Matthew played with a dreamy look on his face. I couldn't tell if he was good or not, but he certainly seemed to be enjoying himself.

After the rehearsal the conductor asked Third Sister to stay behind and play a short piece for him. I waited for her outside so we could go home together.

Matthew came up to me while I was waiting. "I heard your sister tell the conductor that your father is a violin teacher."

"Yes, he is," I answered. Maybe this was a chance to get Father another student? "Do you want to take lessons?"

Matthew looked very uncomfortable. "I'd really like to, but my folks can't afford it."

"My father is cheap," I said eagerly, although I didn't actually know how much Father charged. But I felt sure he would love to have a new student, especially someone who really liked music.

When Third Sister came out, she was smiling. "The conductor wants me to play a solo for our first concert!"

I was very happy for her, and even Matthew looked glad. "Hey, that's great!" he said.

"This is my stand partner, Matthew," I said. "And this is my third sister —"

"Hi, my name is Mary," interrupted Third Sister.

I stared at her. I didn't even know she had an American name. She must have picked it without telling the rest of the family. Maybe she felt it would be easier for her new friends to remember.

I'd noticed that many Americans had trouble with Chinese names. When I told people my name was Yingtao, they always asked me to spell it. Even after I spelled it, they had trouble re-membering it.

"I heard you play just now," Matthew said to Third Sister. "You're really good!"

Third Sister dimpled again. "I'm terrible. You're just saying that to be nice."

She didn't mean it, of course. That's the way my parents taught us to answer when someone praises us.

26

"Well, I guess I'd better run," said Matthew. But he didn't seem in a hurry to go.

Neither was Third Sister eager to have him go — not when he had just told her how much he admired her playing. "Would you like to come to our house and meet my elder brother and sister? They also play musical instruments."

Matthew grinned. "Sure, if it's okay with your folks."

"My parents would be glad to meet one of Fourth Brother's friends," she told him.

I liked the way she said that — as if Matthew was really my friend, as if I had lots of other friends.

My parents weren't home, but we found Second Sister in the kitchen, cutting tea bags. "This is my other sister," I told him. "She plays the viola."

Second Sister looked a little moody but not too moody to greet Matthew politely with "Hello."

I waited to see if she had chosen an American name, too. But she just picked up her scissors again.

As we went up the stairs, Matthew looked at me. "What was your sister doing in the kitchen?

It looked like she was cutting up tea bags."

"She was."

At the landing Matthew stopped and looked at me again. "What for?"

I was used to seeing Second Sister cutting tea bags, and it had never occurred to me that it might look funny. "When we make tea, we put some tea leaves in the bottom of the cup, and pour hot water over them," I said. "It's ready to drink when all the leaves are wet and sink to the bottom."

"But why do you need to cut the bags?"

"Well, my mother saw some tea for sale at the market one day, and she bought a big box. But it turned out to be all tea bags, not loose tea. So Second Sister cuts up a few bags every day and pours the loose tea into a jar."

It was perfectly obvious to me that tea would steep better when it's loose than when it's tightly packed into a tiny bag.

But I guess Matthew didn't think so. He was still shaking his head and looking puzzled.

I opened the door to the room I shared with Eldest Brother. He was inside, sitting on the floor and screwing knobs into the ends of orange crates. Beside him were a couple of boards and some bricks.

I introduced Matthew, who looked wide-eyed at the crates and boards. "What are you making?"

"I'm making a chest of drawers," said Eldest Brother. "The boards will sit over the piles of bricks to make a top, and the orange crates are the drawers. The knobs make it easier to pull them out."

Matthew peered into one of the crates, which already contained my shirts and underwear. "Why don't you put your clothes in a regular dresser?"

"We don't have enough money to buy much furniture," explained Eldest Brother.

"Gee, I'm sorry," Matthew said, turning red. "I didn't mean to sound rude or nosy." For some reason, he was very sensitive about money.

I had to show Matthew that we didn't mind. Chinese people aren't at all embarrassed to talk about money. When we meet someone, we often ask him how much money he makes.

"That's okay," I told Matthew. "I don't think you're rude or nosy at all."

"My mother was glad when she found all these orange crates she could have for free," Elder Brother said.

As he continued to put the knobs in, I told him that Matthew loved music.

29

Elder Brother looked pleased. "Are you in the school orchestra?"

"I play the violin," answered Matthew. "I'm Yingtao's stand partner."

Eldest Brother stopped smiling. "Did the conductor put you there after the audition?"

I knew why he asked that. He was trying to find out if Matthew was my stand partner because he played as badly as I did.

"I'm a beginner," said Matthew. "I only started playing the violin last fall. The school had an extra violin that nobody else was using, so I asked if I could borrow it."

"Do you take lessons?" asked Eldest Brother.

Again Matthew turned red. "My parents can't afford them," he mumbled. "My father is out of work right now."

I suddenly had an idea. "Maybe you can give him some free lessons," I said to Eldest Brother. "They don't have to be more than fifteen minutes, just long enough to show him what he's doing wrong."

Eldest Brother looked thoughtful. Finally he got up and went to his violin case. "Play something," he said, taking out the instrument and handing it to Matthew.

Matthew swallowed and wiped his hands on

30

his pants. Then he took the violin carefully and looked at it with wide eyes. "Wow," he breathed. "This is beautiful!"

He closed his eyes for a minute and then began to play. From the expression on Eldest Brother's face, I knew that he liked the sound of what he was hearing.

When Matthew finished, Eldest Brother stood silent and then smiled. "It's certainly clear that you have not been playing very long. But you have a nice feel for the violin."

Matthew looked almost scared. "Then . . . then . . ."

Eldest Brother smiled more widely. "All right, I'll give you lessons. We can start after dinner tonight, if you want. Why don't you stay and eat with us?"

Matthew accepted and went to phone his parents for permission. When he came back he asked if he could go to the bathroom.

I was surprised. Did Americans always take a bath before dinner?

"Is it all right if you didn't take a bath just now?" I asked him. "Our tub has something in it."

It was Matthew's turn to look surprised. "I don't need a bath."

31

"Then why did you tell me you wanted one?" I demanded.

"I just want to go to the toilet," he explained. He began to laugh. "And you thought I actually asked to take a bath? Without someone making me?"

I laughed, too. This was not like Jake and the others laughing at me for standing at attention when the teacher came in. We were laughing together because we were sharing a joke. I began to like Matthew very much.

When he came out of the bathroom, he looked shocked. "Was I seeing things, or were there really fish swimming in your bathtub?"

"That's just some carp my mother bought in Chinatown today. We're having them for dinner tonight."

"But they're alive!"

"Of course they're alive!" I snorted. "My mother would never buy dead fish. They're not fresh."

"I've never had live fish," Matthew said, as we went downstairs. "The fish I eat are nice and dead. They come in a can, or they're frozen sticks covered with bread crumbs."

When we came into the dining room, Matthew was muttering, " . . . cut-up tea bags,

32

knobs on orange crates, fish in the bathtub . . ."

"Does your friend always talk to himself?" whispered Second Sister as I helped her set the table.

I just smiled. It was a good thing that Second Sister couldn't hear what he was saying.

Matthew was our first American dinner guest. Father nodded approval when Eldest Brother introduced him as my friend and said he had a very good ear.

When we eat dinner, we normally help ourselves to food from the platters in the middle of the table. But since Matthew was my guest, I acted as a host and served him with food.

After a while I noticed that he wasn't eating much. He spent most of the time staring at the chopsticks in my right hand.

"What's wrong?" I asked.

"I've never used chopsticks before," he admitted sheepishly.

"Why don't you give him a fork, Yingtao?" suggested Mother.

"No, please," Matthew said quickly. "I really want to learn how to use chopsticks."

So I taught him. I showed him how to grip one of the two sticks steady and jiggle the other stick to close down on a piece of meat.

33

He managed to eat most of the food I served him, but I noticed he didn't eat much of the fish. "I'm not used to eating someone I saw

34

swimming just a little while ago," he whispered
apologetically.

Matthew learned fast, and by the end of the

meal he was using chopsticks pretty well. "Hey, this is good finger exercise!" he joked. "I bet it's going to help my violin playing."

"If that's true, then why doesn't Fourth Brother play a little better?" sniffed Second Sister. "He's been using chopsticks since he was two years old!"

Matthew gave me a sympathetic smile. I was used to remarks from the family about my violin playing, but it was still nice to have someone who was on my side.

3

From that day on Matthew was my best friend. I didn't have to stand by myself at recess anymore, and we helped each other a lot in school.

I was able to help Matthew with his math homework. Chinese schools are ahead of American schools in math, so everybody thought I was a math genius when I always finished my work long before anyone else. Matthew told me that most kids hated math, except those who were geniuses.

I'm certainly no genius, and Third Sister is much better at math than I am. But I was happy to have people think I was good at something, so I didn't say anything.

Matthew helped me with spelling. I had a lot of trouble because English just didn't sound the

37

way it looked. So Matthew drilled me on tough words like "cough," "enough," and "dough."

I was getting used to American schools. Not only did I stop jumping to attention when the teacher came into the room, I began to slouch in my seat like the other kids. Once I even interrupted to ask a question. In China, the only time we would interrupt the teacher would be if the building was on fire or one of the students was having a fit.

I began to eat lunch with Matthew and his friends. Third Sister looked relieved, because now she could sit and eat with her own friends.

Some of the boys made fun of my lunch, because I'd bring sandwiches with fillings like stir-fried bean sprouts. At first Matthew got angry when his friends laughed, but he soon saw that I didn't mind too much.

"Doesn't it bother you that those guys are always bugging you?" he asked afterward.

"No, it's okay," I said. "I'm used to it. I get a lot of it at home."

"You know, you're tough, Yingtao — a lot tougher than you look."

There was real admiration in his voice, and I suddenly felt twice as tall. There I was, Yang the scrawny, Yang the youngest, and my friend was telling me I was tough.

Just before our spring vacation, we had an assembly. All the classes in the school went into a huge auditorium, and we heard speeches by public officials. We had a lot of speeches in China, too, but they were different. Once I tried to tell Matthew, Jake and the others about the political speeches we had in China. But they didn't understand when I tried to explain. Maybe it was because I didn't understand, myself.

Our orchestra also played some pieces, and several players had solos, including Third Sister. But what I liked best on the program were the funny skits put on by the fifth grade students. In one of them, a tall boy sang a song in a high voice, just like a girl's. Then it turned out that he was only moving his lips, while a girl hiding behind a screen was doing the real singing. Matthew told me afterward that this was called lip sync.

After school one day, Matthew took me to a field nearby to watch him play baseball with the neighborhood boys' team. Before they started playing the game, they spent some time throwing the ball around. Matthew suddenly turned and threw the ball at me.

Without even thinking, I stretched out my arm and caught it. I loved the feeling of the ball smacking against my hand.

"Great catch!" cried the other boys.

I was so happy that I just stood there with a big grin on my face.

The coach came up to us and said, "Matthew, why don't you ask your friend if he'd like to play? Jerry can't come today."

"Sure," said Matthew happily. "I think Ying-tao is dying to play." He turned to me. "Here, take my bat and go up to the plate."

For a second I just stared at him.

A bat is a small flying animal that is supposed to bring good luck, I thought. I looked at the big stick Matthew held out to me. Was this a bat, too?

I took the stick and looked around for the plate. We didn't use dinner plates in China, but I had eaten Western meals before, and I knew what plates looked like: big, flat, shiny, round things made of china (but not always from China).

"What are you waiting for?" asked the boy who was catcher. "Get over here!" He pointed to a spot in front of him on the ground, which was outlined in white chalk.

So that was the plate. It was hard enough to learn English, and now I was discovering that English words meant something completely different in baseball language. But I had to learn it if I wanted to play.

The pitcher stared at me for a moment, raised one leg high in the air, and suddenly threw the ball hard at me.

The ball shrank in size and looked no bigger than a walnut. How could I possibly hit that tiny thing?

Trying to remember what the other batters had done, I swung my bat furiously. I missed completely, and nearly lost my balance.

"Strike!" called the man who seemed to be acting as judge.

Strike? Why did he call it a strike? I hadn't struck the ball at all. I had missed. It didn't make sense at all.

The pitcher threw again. I could see that the ball was coming too low for me to hit it well, so I didn't even try to swing the bat.

"Ball!" called the judge.

Of course it was a ball. It was round, and besides, what else did you use in baseball? The judge didn't have to tell me. While I was still trying to make sense out of what was happening, the pitcher threw a ball at me again.

"Strike!" said the judge.

Did the judge have trouble with his eyes? Maybe he needed glasses. But to my surprise, everybody else seemed to agree with him. I was totally confused.

Again the pitcher threw while I was not ready, and again the judge yelled "Ball!"

I pulled myself together, and when the next ball came, I swung my bat hard. I heard a beautiful crack and knew that I had hit the ball at last. But the ball flew high up in the air and was caught by one of the players on the other team.

"Out!" cried the judge. I didn't need to be told what that meant.

Matthew came over and, to my surprise, told me that I had done well. "You could tell that ball was low, couldn't you?" he said. "I bet you'll make a great batter someday."

"Yeah, all he needs is a little practice," said another boy. Suddenly I found myself surrounded by people who actually approved of me. For an instant, I even thought I saw Eldest

Brother among the others. But it turned out to be just an American boy who was slender and had black hair.

It was still wonderful to have people smiling at something I had done, instead of screwing up their faces with pain. I felt like floating away into the sky. I had often seen a happy, floating-away look on Eldest Brother's face when he played a piece he really liked. I had never thought I'd feel it myself.

From that day on, instead of walking home after school with Third Sister, I began to stop by the field with Matthew and practice baseball as often as I could. I felt a little guilty about it, because I knew I should have been spending the time practicing my violin. But I didn't feel *too* guilty, because I knew that it didn't make much difference whether I practiced or not. Third Sister knew how much I enjoyed baseball, and she didn't tell on me.

But I couldn't keep the baseball playing a secret. During one of my lessons with Father, he noticed that I was holding my bow differently. "What happened to your hand?" he asked, pointing to my knuckles, which were raw.

"I scraped my hand sliding on the ground," I mumbled. One of the other players had taught me how to slide in the dirt and to touch the home plate before the ball could reach the catcher.

Father frowned. "And just why have you been sliding on the ground?"

Bit by bit the truth came out. I had to tell him about baseball, about going to the field after school and playing on the neighborhood team.

I was afraid Father would be very angry. Instead, he looked sad. "Yingtao, your mother and I both know that you are less fond of music than your brother and sisters. It's clear that your heart isn't in your playing. But why don't you at least try harder — just this once, just for the recital? It's very important to me. It's important to our whole family."

He was begging. I hated to see Father like this. I'd rather have him shouting at me.

How could I tell him that with or without scraped knuckles, I would play miserably — that no matter how hard I tried, I simply could not play in tune? In our string quartet, I was about as useful as a rickshaw with one wheel.

It wouldn't be so bad if we weren't playing a string quartet. When I played in the orchestra or sang in a chorus, I had my usual ways to escape. But in a string quartet, there was no escape, no way for me to cover up.

"Father, why do you make us play a string quartet in the recital?" I asked. "Why can't you just have Eldest Brother play a solo?"

Father thought for a moment before answering my question. "I'll tell you why, Yingtao. When you're playing a solo piece, you care only about yourself. When you're playing in a large orchestra, you do what everyone else is doing. But in a quartet, you have to cooperate with the others, and at the same time you speak out for yourself. Each voice is heard. That's why I love string quartets best of all the different kinds of music."

I knew that he believed in letting each person speak out, in letting each voice be heard. We had heard him say it often. In China not everybody agreed with him. Once I overheard Mother telling him to be careful when he said that.

In most Chinese families, usually the father makes all the decisions and the rest silently accept them. But in our house Father would encourage us to speak out and let each voice in the family be heard. We loved him for it.

But it was because I loved him so much that I couldn't speak out. I knew that if I told him I hated the violin, it would hurt him deeply. The trouble is, in this case we would really be better off if the voice of my violin *couldn't* be heard.

After he started lessons from Eldest Brother, Matthew improved very fast. But in the school orchestra, he still sat with me in the back row, where the worst players were. The conductor was too busy to notice Matthew's improvement, and until there was another audition for all the players, Matthew would have to stay where he was.

He didn't say anything about it, but I knew he wanted some proof that he was getting better.

"My brother says that after only one month of lessons, you're already playing better than I did after four years of lessons," I told him.

He didn't look convinced. "Your brother was just being nice. My folks still hate the sound of my fiddle."

My family was getting used to having Matthew eat with us. By the time his lesson with Elder Brother was finished, it was often dinnertime already.

Matthew began to be embarrassed. "I'm eating dinner at your house a lot, lately. And I'm getting free music lessons, too."

"That's all right," I said. "We often have guests for dinner. We just set some extra plates and chopsticks and add water to the soup."

"But how do you know if you'll have enough food to go around?"

"Everybody just eats a little less. We can always fill up on rice."

"You must run out of rice a lot then," said Matthew.

He was right. We needed more rice that very afternoon. Usually, Second Sister went shopping with Mother, but she was in one of her moods today.

"Matthew and I can go and carry for you," I said to Mother.

Looking first at me and then at Matthew, Mother smiled. "Since there are two of you to help carry, I'll buy a big sack of rice this time — a fifty-pound bag."

Even with the two of us, we were panting hard when we finally heaved the sack of rice into the bus. Matthew didn't believe me at first when I told him that we would eat up all the rice in about two months.

"Gee, I don't know how you stay so skinny when you eat so much!" he said.

"Hey, Matthew!" somebody yelled when we had entered the bus and arranged the sack of rice at our feet. "What have you got there? Cement?"

It was Jake, the boy who had taken my pen during recess at school. He came over to look at the sack. "Phoenix Brand Fragrant Rice, fifty pounds," he said, reading the label.

Then he grinned. "If you eat all this, Matthew, the curl will go out of your hair, and you'll have straight black hair like your Chinese friend here."

Jake went back to his friends at the back of the bus, and I heard laughter.

Matthew pretended not to hear, but his face turned a little red. For the first time, I realized that being friends with me could be embarrassing for him.

But that didn't stop Matthew from staying to dinner that evening. He was using chopsticks pretty well by now, and he only dropped a few things on the table. He even ate a little fish.

Matthew looked up from his fish bones. "Can

49

I stay around and listen to the quartet practice tonight?" he asked Father.

"Of course you can!" said Father, looking pleased. He turned to me. "See how serious your friend is about music, Yingtao. You can learn from his example."

"Maybe he can even play your part in the quartet for a little while," suggested Mother. "Then you can hear how it's *supposed* to sound."

Mother didn't say this to be cruel. She really thought it would improve my "attitude." Except for Third Sister, everybody in the family had been saying things like this for years. I should have been used to it, but somehow it felt worse when they said it in front of my friend.

So Matthew stayed in the living room with us while we set up the stands and put out the music for the quartet.

As usual we had to stop after playing only a few bars, and the place where we stopped was the place where I started playing. Eldest Brother screwed up his face. He looked like someone who had bitten into a green persimmon.

I glanced at Matthew and saw the same suffering on his face, although he tried not to show it. For a moment I felt bad. Even my best friend couldn't stand my playing.

50

Oh, well, if my own brother and sisters couldn't bear to listen, how could I expect a friend to?

Then, Second Sister remembered Mother's suggestion. "Fourth Brother, why don't you let Matthew play the second violin part? Just so that you get an idea."

I got up and let him take my seat. Standing by myself in a corner, I watched the four of them start to play.

At first Matthew made some mistakes, mostly in counting time. The music was new to him, after all. But he learned quickly, and soon he was playing away. I saw Eldest Brother nod. Even his fussy ear was satisfied.

It was true that Matthew's curly brown hair looked funny, surrounded by the straight black hair of the Yangs. But as Jake had said in the bus, maybe if he ate enough rice . . .

Suddenly I felt an ache in my chest. I wasn't exactly jealous of Matthew — after all, he was my best friend, and I was the one who had invited him over. But I felt left out.

After that, Matthew came regularly to our rehearsals. Second Sister would stop the playing after about ten bars into the quartet. "Why don't you let Matthew take over, Fourth Brother," she would say. "Then you can hear how your part is supposed to sound."

So Matthew ended up playing the second violin part most of the time. None of the others objected.

Then one day, he told me in school that he wouldn't be able to come to my house that afternoon for his lesson with Elder Brother.

"My parents think that I'm spending too much time at your house," he said.

"What's wrong with that?" I asked. Then an uncomfortable thought struck me. "Is it because we're Chinese?"

"No, of course not!" Matthew said quickly — maybe too quickly? "See, I'm eating dinner with you a couple of times a week already, and my mom is embarrassed about that."

"She doesn't have to be," I told him. "We still have about thirty pounds of rice left. And you can help me carry another fifty-pound sack if we run out."

Matthew shook his head. "I don't know. But I'll work on my mom and try to change her mind."

A couple of days later he said his parents had invited me over to dinner at his house.

I suspected they wanted to look me over. I knew that when I went to Matthew's house that evening, I had to make a really good impression.

4

Mr. Conner, Matthew's father, opened the door. "Hello, you must be . . . uh . . ." He turned to Matthew.

"This is Yingtao," said Matthew.

"Sorry," said Mr. Conner. "I have a hard time with Chinese names."

"That's okay," I told him. "I have a hard time with American names."

Mr. Conner looked startled. Maybe he wasn't expecting me to speak whole sentences.

"Your mom's getting some groceries," he said to Matthew. "Supper will be a little late."

"Come on, let's go to my room," Matthew said to me.

"Shouldn't we go to the store and help your mother carry the groceries home?" I asked.

54

"It's all right," said Matthew. "Mom's driving."

I was surprised. Since Matthew had told me that his father had lost his job and couldn't afford to pay for music lessons, I expected the Conner family to be really poor. "Your family can afford to drive a car?" I asked.

Now Matthew looked surprised. "Of course. Everybody drives."

"In China, only officials and executives of big companies have cars," I told him.

The Conners certainly didn't look poor. Their house was made of wood, painted in a nice light blue color, and it had a yard both in front and in back, with neatly cut lawns.

"Do you share your house with another family?" I asked.

Matthew shook his head. "Nope. We have it all to ourselves. Eric and I each have our own room."

I looked around in wonder at the spacious living room with its matching sofa and armchairs, and at the dining room, which had a table, matching dining chairs, and cupboards.

"I really like your house," I told Matthew.

Matthew looked pleased. "Dad bought this house cheap and fixed it up. Eric and I helped him."

I was impressed. "You really helped him with the carpentry work?"

"Well, we mostly handed him his tools," admitted Matthew. "But he did let us pound a few nails."

I couldn't imagine Father working on a house. In China, when something needed to be done in our apartment, we just called in a carpenter. We even had a carpenter come in to make beds for us. It was cheaper than buying ready-made beds. After we came to America, Eldest Brother got a hammer and did a little repair work, but I didn't think he would ask me to help him.

"It must be nice to help your father fix up your own house," I said wistfully. "We're renting, and we can afford only half of a house. We all have to double up in the bedrooms."

"Well, that's because you're newcomers to this country," said Matthew. "I bet you had more room back in China."

I nearly laughed. "In China, all four of us had to share one bedroom. We ate our meals in the living room, and that's where my parents slept at night. At least we were lucky and had our own kitchen."

"You mean some apartments don't have their own kitchens?" asked Matthew, surprised.

"Most of them don't. Many of our friends had to share a kitchen with two or even four other families. We had to share a bathroom and toilet with our neighbors across the hall."

Matthew looked stunned. "But . . . but . . . your brother has that beautiful violin. You all have expensive instruments. Your family can't be that hard up!"

"We *have* to have good instruments," I said. "According to Father, you can't make good music without good instruments."

But you can have a good instrument and still make terrible music, I said to myself. Matthew was silent and thoughtful as we went up the stairs to his room.

I found his room filled with furniture. Besides a bed, he had a bookshelf, a desk, and a chest with six drawers. The windows even had cloth curtains with ruffles.

In the room I shared with Elder Brother, there were only rolled shades. We pulled them down when the sun was in our eyes, but they would roll up with a loud snap, especially when I was practicing. I still couldn't get used to them.

I went around, admiring Matthew's room. The walls were almost completely covered with photographs. They were divided into two kinds:

57

pictures of baseball players and pictures of violinists.

It was funny, seeing the photo of a ballplayer in his uniform holding a bat, and next to it the photo of a musician in a tuxedo holding a violin and a bow. I laughed.

"You're just like my brother Eric," grumbled Matthew. "He thinks you can't be a baseball fan and a music fan at the same time."

Matthew looked annoyed, so I changed the subject and asked him about his father. "What did your father do before he lost his job?"

"He was a machinist," said Matthew. "He got laid off when his company shut down one of their plants here."

"Laid off? Was he hurt badly?"

Matthew looked puzzled. "I didn't say he was hurt."

"But . . . but . . . I thought he was laid off on a stretcher or something."

"Oh boy, here we go again," said Matthew. He took a deep breath. " 'Laid off' doesn't have anything to do with lying down. It's another way of saying he lost his job."

"Oh. That's too bad. How long ago did he get . . . er . . . laid off?"

"It's been more than two months now."

58

"No wonder you don't have money for music lessons," I said. Matthew had been surprised because we had expensive instruments, but no money for furniture. The Conners had a big, beautiful house full of furniture, but no money for music lessons. Did they have money for food?

I started to worry about dinner. Somehow I didn't think the Conners bought fifty-pound bags of rice. "Will you have enough food tonight if I eat here?"

"Look, we're not exactly starving around here!" Matthew looked a little offended by my question, and also by my reminder that he didn't have enough money for music lessons.

"I'm sorry," I said quickly. "I didn't mean . . ."

"No, that's okay. Dad has unemployment benefits, and Mom has a part-time job. Besides, both Eric and I have paper routes."

"A paper route." I chewed over the words. Sometimes, if I say the words very, very slowly, they begin to make sense. But not this time.

Matthew explained. "A paper route means delivering newspapers. Every morning we go around and throw newspapers on people's front porches. We do it before going to school."

"That means you have to get up early in the morning," I said, feeling sorry for him. I felt sorry for anyone who had to get up early.

Matthew shrugged. "It's not too bad. Eric and I make good money. We earn enough to buy our own clothes and games and stuff."

He looked at me curiously. "Don't you guys work? How about your sisters? Do they make any money baby-sitting?"

"Baby-sitting?"

"You know, sit babies, when their parents go out," Matthew said patiently — maybe too patiently.

Talking to Americans is like walking along a country footpath in China. You think the path is nice and firm, but your foot suddenly slips on a muddy stretch and you land with a big splash in a wet rice paddy.

My family tries hard to study English. Whenever we come across a strange word, we look it up in a dictionary. But knowing what each word means isn't always enough.

"You mean sit a baby down on a chair?" I finally asked Matthew. "Why should my sisters earn any money doing that?"

Matthew tugged at his hair. He did this a lot when we talked together. Another thing he did

60

was to take a few deep breaths. He did this now. "Forget it. Do you and your brother and sisters earn any money?"

"Why should we?" I asked, puzzled. "We've got enough to eat, and we have a nice apartment. It's not as nice as your house, but it's good enough for us."

Matthew looked really shocked.

"Everybody needs some spending money! I mean, you can't beg your parents for money every time you go to the movies, or something."

I began to feel uncomfortable. "It's true we ask our parents for money if we want to go to the movies. But we don't go a lot, and we don't really go down on our knees to beg."

"In America, most kids get a job and earn their own pocket money. Besides, it helps their parents out."

"We can't get a job," I said. "We're still going to school."

"Yeah? Well, Eric and I go to school, too. I mean, don't you earn money in your extra time?"

"We spend all our extra time studying and practicing music. We don't have any time left for jobs."

Matthew frowned. "I guess that's why my dad

61

doesn't want me to take music lessons. It's not just the money. Maybe he thinks practicing music wastes too much time."

My parents believed that practicing music was never a waste of time. In my case they were wrong, but nothing could change their minds.

Before we could say any more, a boy's voice called, "Supper's ready!"

We ran downstairs. I was introduced to Mrs. Conner, who looked tired. She brushed a damp curl from her forehead, smiled quickly, and began to carry dishes of food from the kitchen.

"Aw, not tuna casserole again!" said Eric, Matthew's older brother.

"Say hello to Matthew's friend," growled Mr. Conner.

Eric rolled his eyes, but he did say "Hi" to me. Then he went back to glaring at the tuna dish in the middle of the table.

I couldn't understand why Eric didn't like tuna. I found it delicious. Seafood is expensive in China, and I like it better than meat. I hoped that Mrs. Conner didn't have to spend a lot of money on the dinner — not when Mr. Conner was out of work, not when Matthew didn't have money for music lessons.

There wasn't much talk at the dinner table. Mr. Conner ate slowly but deliberately. I remembered that Matthew had said his father was a machinist. Maybe he liked things to work smoothly. Mrs. Conner was busy passing the dishes of food around.

I felt the eyes of the whole Conner family on me, and I knew they were waiting to see if I'd do something funny, like bringing the salad bowl to my mouth and drinking up the dressing left at the bottom.

In fact that was what I had tried to do the first time we went to McDonald's and had their salad. But Mother had stopped me. When we got home, she gave us all a lesson in the proper way to eat in America. She also bought us a book on etiquette.

At least learning to eat in America was a lot easier than learning to talk. We learned how to use a knife and fork, not to slurp the spaghetti, not to hunch over the dinner plate, and so on. We just followed the rules. It's not like talking, when you carefully look up new words in a dictionary, and still fall into traps about being laid off and baby-sitting.

At first the Conners looked a little disap-

pointed when I didn't do anything strange. But after a while I saw them relax, and soon they began to chat.

Eric picked out the green peas in the tuna dish. "Matthew told me you ate live fish," he said to me. "This tuna probably looks pretty tame to you."

"Live fish?" I didn't know what he meant.

64

"Live carp," he said, "that you scoop up from your bathtub."

"Eric, the carp was alive in the tub, but they cooked it afterward," said Matthew, his face turning red. "Why don't you ever listen?"

I enjoyed hearing the phrase "Why don't you ever listen?" being said to somebody else for a change. Did Eric have a terrible ear, too?

I was also a little surprised that Matthew had spoken that way to Eric, his elder brother. In our family, I had to speak respectfully to Eldest Brother, Second Sister, and Third Sister, although they could all be insulting to me, the youngest Yang.

But Eric only scowled at his younger brother and went back to picking out peas.

Mr. Conner turned to me. "Matthew says your family is really musical."

"Not me," I said. "I'm terrible at music."

"I'm sure you're just being modest," said Mrs. Conner.

"No, he really is awful," said Matthew. "He's probably the worst player in our orchestra — and that's saying a lot!"

"Matthew!" said his mother. "That's no way to talk about your friend!"

I had to show them I wasn't angry. "Matthew is right. I have a terrible ear. I wish I never had to touch my violin again."

Mr. Conner looked up from his plate. "Is that a fact? Then why do you play?"

"My parents make me," I mumbled.

"Oh, you poor thing," said Mrs. Conner. Her eyes were warm with sympathy. "Here, have some more tuna casserole."

Even Eric seemed more friendly. "If you don't like music, what do you like?"

"When I went to school in China, what I liked best was gymnastics."

I had never said this to my family. And here, on my very first visit, I was telling the Conners.

Eric made a face. "Gymnastics? It's mostly girls who go in for that."

"I like other sports, too," I said. "Matthew took me to watch him and his friends play baseball. I even play sometimes. It's really fun."

Mr. Conner smiled. "Hey, that's great. Baseball is our national sport. If you like baseball, you'll be right at home here."

He turned to Matthew. "I'm glad you made friends with . . . uh . . ."

"Yingtao," I supplied.

"Yeah, with Yingtao. A boy should have lots of different interests and not spend all his time on music."

Mrs. Conner smiled, too. "We were getting embarrassed because Matthew was eating dinner at your house so much. I'm glad you could come over here for a change."

"Maybe we can go out in the yard and hit a few balls later," Eric said to me.

After dinner Matthew helped his mother wash the dishes. I started to join them.

"Guests don't have to do the dishes," said Eric. "Come on, let's go outside."

Eric brought his baseball out into the yard, and we began to practice throwing.

"Hey, not bad!" he said, when I jumped up to catch a throw that almost sailed into the neighbor's yard.

"Matthew taught me how to do that," I said.

At the mention of his brother, Eric made a face. "Matthew is no fun anymore, now that he's into music."

I wasn't quite sure what he meant. "Why not? You mean he's too busy to play with you?"

Eric looked at his feet. "He looks like such a nerd, carrying that violin case around!"

"What's a nerd?" This word hadn't come up on any of Third Sister's lists.

"A nerd is . . . well, a wimp."

"What's a wimp?" That was another word not on Third Sister's lists.

Eric tugged at his hair. Maybe this was a habit that ran in the Conner family. "It's . . . it's kind of a sissy."

Finally a word I knew. A sissy was someone who was afraid of everything. Matthew was one of the bigger boys in our class, and I had never seen him looking afraid. "I don't think Matthew is a sissy at all."

"The other kids laugh and call him Matthew the Boy Genius," muttered Eric.

"I'm sure what the other kids say doesn't bother Matthew," I told Eric.

"Well, it bothers *me*," grumbled Eric. "And it bothers my dad, too."

I had learned something. In America, it seemed that playing a violin made a boy a nerd, a wimp, a sissy.

"My elder brother and I both play the violin," I said.

Eric shuffled his feet. "That's different. You're Chinese. Everybody knows Chinese kids do that kind of thing — you know — study hard, play the violin."

"Does that mean Chinese kids are all nerds?"

"Not you!" Eric said quickly. "You're all right."

"My folks liked you," Matthew told me later as I was getting ready to leave. "Now that they've met you, they aren't worried anymore."

I was puzzled. "Why were they worried?"

Matthew looked away. "I guess they were afraid that I'd get even more involved with music if I went to your house so much. But you told them you liked sports, so now they think you're okay."

I had passed the test. Matthew's parents thought I was good for him.

"You know, you're really lucky!" Matthew said suddenly.

I was surprised. "You're the one who's lucky. You're musical. My brother says so, and so does my father."

"But at *your* house, people are happy when you make music," Matthew said in a low voice. "At *my* house, people say, 'Oh, not that again!' when I play my violin."

"At my house, people are *not* happy when I make music," I said. "People say, 'Oh, not that again!' when *I'm* the one who is playing the violin."

We looked at each other. "Too bad we can't trade places," sighed Matthew.

That was when I had my brilliant idea. "Maybe," I said slowly, "we can."

5

Lip sync, that was the idea. Only it wouldn't be lip sync, but bow sync. Matthew would hide behind a screen at the recital and play my part while I moved my bow back and forth silently.

Matthew was shocked when I told him about my idea. "Sure, I want to help you, Yingtao, but this is crazy! We'll never get away with it!"

"It's not crazy," I insisted. "I've had lots of practice moving my bow in time to the music. Don't you want to play in the quartet? This is your chance."

It took a while, but I finally convinced him.

He even began to look excited. "If I can perform with your brother and sister in a real recital, it'll prove that I'm good," he said softly. Lately Matthew had sounded discouraged because in

71

the school orchestra he was still seated next to me, in the very last row.

"You must know by now that you're talented," I said. "My brother and sisters all say so."

"They're just saying that to be nice," he muttered.

"Then why can't they tell *me* I'm talented and be nice to me, too?" I demanded.

Matthew grinned. "Because they know you wouldn't believe them." He became serious. "Maybe they keep saying how good I am to make you work harder, to improve your so-called attitude."

"Well, if that's what you believe," I said quickly, "then you should certainly play in the recital. It will be a test, sort of." I added, "But you can't tell anyone."

"No, but I'll prove something to *myself*," he said. "That's all I care about."

Looking at his shining eyes, I knew that Matthew really loved music. He didn't play to impress an audience, to hear people clapping for him. He would play his heart out even if nobody could see him.

This was what a real music lover was like. I remembered the times when Eldest Brother played a piece alone in his room, not to practice for a lesson or a recital — just because he enjoyed playing.

Since Matthew had already been practicing the second violin part of the quartet, he didn't even need to rehearse with the others. All we had to do was arrange for him to play in the recital itself.

First, we needed a screen to hide him — and I knew just what we could use. Mother had bought an old folding screen at a garage sale, and she was planning to fix it up and use it to divide our dining area from the living room.

"You know the screen you bought last week?" I said to Mother. "Can we use it for the recital?"

"What for?" she asked. "It needs paint, and one of the hinges is broken."

"It'll look more like a stage that way," I said. "Don't we want things to look nice?"

Second Sister sniffed. "Why don't you worry less about the look of the recital and more about the sound?"

When I told Matthew about using the screen, he thought for a moment. "Maybe Mary can help us sell the idea of a screen to your family," he said finally.

"Who's Mary?" I asked, puzzled.

He stared at me. "Who's Mary? How can you forget your own sister's name?"

In fact I had forgotten my sister's name. Third Sister hadn't told the rest of the family that she had chosen the English name of Mary, and she was called that only by her friends at school.

I guess Second Sister was too proud to change her name in order to join the crowd. Unlike Third Sister, who had already changed her haircut to look more like the other girls in school, Second Sister still wore her hair in two long braids, exactly the way she had done in China.

I agreed with Matthew that it would be a good idea to get Third Sister's help. The very next day after school, we talked to her about our plan. As we had hoped, she approved.

"You're right, this is our only way to save the recital." Then she added, "You can't make a silk purse out of a sow's ear."

These days Third Sister wasn't satisfied with learning five new words every day. She was beginning to make lists of whole new sentences that would be useful.

I didn't understand, and she had to explain that she meant we could never make a tone-deaf person (a sow's ear) into a violinist (a silk purse).

74

Maybe I had a terrible ear, but I thought that comparing me to a sow was not very kind.

The important thing, though, was that Third Sister helped us to convince the family. She announced that we should have a pair of Chinese scenes painted on the folding screen.

That got Second Sister interested. She was the best one in the family with the Chinese brush, and she offered to do some brush paintings.

Even Mother liked the idea. "Some Chinese pictures would make a fine background. If we do a good job, we can use the screen for all our future recitals."

Using a thick Chinese brush and black ink, Second Sister painted two long and narrow pictures, one for each panel of the screen. The first one showed some rocky mountains covered with pine trees, and the second one showed a little boat going down the river.

I was surprised at how much time she spent on the paintings. After school one day, I saw her bent over the dining table, with a long piece of paper spread out in front of her. By her elbow was the inkstone, which we had brought with us from China. It's a flat piece of carved stone, with a depression in the middle. You put a few drops of water in and rub an ink stick against the bottom of the depression until you get a pool of thick, black ink.

Second Sister was holding her brush over the pool of ink, and suddenly I saw a drop of water splash down. It didn't come from the brush. It came from higher up. Another drop plopped into the ink. Second Sister was crying!

Of all the Yangs, she was the most homesick for China. Father was too busy working to support the family, and Mother spent all her time trying to feed us. Eldest Brother was totally wrapped up in his music, and I had Matthew's friendship and baseball to console me. Third Sister already felt at home in America. But Second Sister still missed her old country and her old friends.

She must have heard me come in. She quickly put down her brush and took out a handkerchief to blow her nose.

I tried to find something comforting to say. "I like that picture of the little boat. It reminds me of the time when we went to see the canals in Changzhou."

Second Sister cleared her throat. "I'm surprised you still remember China."

"Of course I do!" I looked away, while she

wiped her eyes. "I'm glad you're painting those pictures. Now we'll always have them to remind us of our old life."

I heard some snuffles. After a moment, Second Sister said huskily, "You're actually a pretty nice boy, Fourth Brother . . ."

Was this the start of a new relationship between us? Would she pick on me a little less from now on?

". . . when you don't have a violin under your chin," she finished.

Oh, well.

After the paintings were done, we all got to work. Eldest Brother put some new screws into the hinges holding the two panels of the screen together. Third Sister and I pasted Second Sister's paintings on the frame.

I had to make sure that Matthew, sitting behind the screen, could see Eldest Brother through the crack where the two panels were joined. He had to be able to see so he could come in together with the others.

Third Sister and I tried out the screen in the living room, and I was glad to find that I could see through the crack.

Matthew said he knew his part and expected to have no trouble with it. Everything seemed to be going well until our parents started to complain.

The trouble was that Matthew and I were spending a lot of time together, both in and out of school. Almost every afternoon, I went to practice baseball after school, and when I was finally accepted as a regular member of the team, it was the proudest moment of my life.

One day Mr. Conner came to the playfield after school. He was substituting for our baseball coach, who was out of town.

"I almost got to play professionally," he told me. "Missed by a hair getting into one of the minor leagues."

He looked so happy, throwing the ball into the air, that I couldn't help grinning. "I'm glad you're here, Mr. Conner."

"Haven't got anything else to do, now that I'm out of work," he growled.

"I hope you can help me with my batting," I said quickly.

"You bet . . . uh . . ."

"Yingtao," I said.

"Yeah, Yingtao. You're keen, and that's what counts. You'll make a great batter someday."

He showed me how to hold my shoulders so I could put all my strength into the swing. I was smaller than the other players, and not as strong, so I could not hit the ball as far as the rest.

But I soon found that I had one talent. I could see exactly how a ball was coming at me: whether it was high, low, off to one side, and whether it was turning as it came — had a spin, as the others said.

This helped me a lot in deciding whether to hit the ball and how to hit it. That's why I was able to get some base hits, although I seldom got a double or a triple. As for a home run, it was an impossible dream.

Matthew's room had pictures of great home run hitters of the past, like Babe Ruth, the Sultan of Swat. But they were mythical figures to me, like the Monkey King in my favorite Chinese story.

Still, even getting just one-base hits, I was counted as a definite plus on our team. The best part was when I came up to bat in the game and saw that the people were looking at me hopefully instead of cringing.

Mr. Conner was delighted when I got a hit that not only put me on first base but sent the boy on third base home. "Good work!" he yelled, and almost jumped up and down in his excitement.

Our team tied the score and needed only one more run to win. Two men were out already, but we had one man on first and one on second.

Matthew came up to bat. He was a good hitter, so we had a real chance to make that run.

The pitcher wound up and threw. Even from where I stood, I could see the ball was high. I wanted to shout to Matthew, "Don't hit it!"

But he swung hard, and the ball flew high into the air. The boy in the outfield caught it easily, and our side was retired.

In the last inning, the other team made another run and won the game. The person who felt the loss most was Mr. Conner.

"Aw, come on, Dad," said Matthew, patting his father on the back. "It's not the end of the world! We've lost before, and we'll probably lose again. We'll probably win again, too."

Mr. Conner shook Matthew's hand off. "Not if you keep on playing like that! You popped that fly because you weren't paying attention! Anybody could've seen that ball was high! Anybody except my musical genius son!"

I tried to distract him. "Is that why Babe Ruth

is called the Sultan of Swat? Because he hit flies?"

Some of the boys laughed, and after a moment, even Mr. Conner had to smile. "A wise guy, huh? Besides making base hits, you make jokes, too?"

But Mr. Conner soon went back to his grumbling. "You know what's wrong with you?" he said to his son. "You're not concentrating."

Walking behind the Conners, I had a strange feeling as I listened to the tone of Mr. Conner's voice. Suddenly it reminded me of *my* father.

The Saturday before the recital, the Conners invited me to go with them to a Mariners game at the Kingdome. My brother and sisters were going to spend the whole weekend practicing, but since practicing wouldn't do me any good, I immediately accepted. Father was at the Seattle Symphony playing in an afternoon concert, and Mother was off shopping. So without asking for permission, I just went.

I enjoyed the game too much to think about the rest of them busy practicing at home. Even though the Mariners lost, it was great to see real professionals playing. This must be how Eldest Brother felt that time in China when he got to hear Isaac Stern play in a concert.

I eagerly watched how the pitcher warmed up, how the batter tested the weight of the bat, how the outfielder ran backward to catch a fly ball.

When I told Mr. Conner afterward how much I loved the game, he was very pleased. "You know how to keep your eyes open, kid. I bet you learned a few things today."

The wonderful feeling from the game disappeared when I walked in our front door. Father had returned and was waiting for me with a stony face. "Where have you been?" he demanded. "Have you forgotten that the recital is only one week away?"

I couldn't meet his eyes. "The Conners invited me to go with them to a baseball game."

Father took a deep breath. "Yingtao," he said finally, "you must know by now that you need the practice more than your brother and your sisters. Don't you care about the recital at all?" He didn't look angry, only terribly sad.

I wanted to tell him that I did care about the recital, that I cared a lot. But he went on. "From now on, there will be no more baseball for you until your violin playing improves."

I crept up to my room. "Until your violin playing improves . . . " This meant that I might never play baseball again.

Matthew was having problems, too. Everybody started calling him "Matthew the Musical Genius." Once Jake said, "Hey, Matthew, why don't you play on street corners, so people can throw coins in your violin case? Think how much money you can make!"

Usually Matthew turned red when he was embarrassed. But this time he turned white. I knew that he was sensitive about money and was very upset because his father wasn't working.

Also, practicing in the quartet cut into his time for baseball. By the time he finally got his homework done, he always went to bed late. Then he had to get up early in the morning to deliver papers.

This made him so sleepy that when he was up at bat, he kept striking out.

"Hey, Matthew, wake up!" the coach would yell at him.

There was worse to come. The team had an important game coming up, and Matthew had forgotten even to show up for practice. I wouldn't have forgotten — ever — but I wasn't there to remind him.

Mr. Conner was furious when Eric told him what had happened. He said that Matthew could not go to our house for more music until his baseball improved.

Since Father had forbidden me to play baseball, I had to get news about the team from Matthew during lunch hour.

"What are we going to do?" asked Matthew. He looked tired, and there were circles under his eyes. I knew he was working too hard. This recital meant as much to him as it did to me. If he didn't get to play, he would be crushed. If he played and played badly, he would be even more crushed.

"You're not getting enough sleep," I said. "Maybe if you didn't have to get up so early in the morning . . ."

"I need the paper route," Matthew said in a low voice. "Our family needs the money."

I knew it upset him to admit that. But why should it? It wasn't his fault, and he couldn't do anything about it.

84

Or could he? With the money they earned, Matthew and Eric paid for their own clothes and school supplies. So they could help their parents quite a lot.

What Matthew had said about his paper route made me thoughtful. Could I earn some money and help my family, too?

Whenever I went grocery shopping with my mother, I noticed that she had to count up all the nickels and dimes carefully. She was always trying to find bargains.

One day she noticed the grocer pulling the green leaves from the broccoli stalks. "What are you going to do with these leaves?" she asked him.

The grocer turned around. "These leaves? We throw them away. They just take up space in the bin, and our customers don't eat them, anyway."

"Then can you give them to me?" asked Mother.

"Sure. You got rabbits or guinea pigs to feed?"

"I've got my family to feed," replied Mother. "These leaves are delicious, and they're full of vitamins."

The grocer was a huge man, and when he looked down at Mother, who was tiny, he grinned. "Tell you what. From now on, I'll save these leaves. Any time you come in, I'll have a bag waiting for you. And if I'm not here, just tell the other grocer that Al wants you to have the broccoli leaves."

Mother had a soft voice, but she somehow got people to do what she wanted. We've been eating free broccoli leaves ever since. To me they taste better than the stalks.

But once when I was helping Mother carry away her usual bags of leaves, I overheard two women talking by the fruit bins.

"Look at those Chinese over there taking away those huge bags of broccoli leaves," said one of them. "Are they really going to eat all that stuff?"

The other one giggled. "I hear that the Chinese will eat almost anything."

It's true that since there are too many people in China and not enough food, we would eat everything that's not a deadly poison. But the two women obviously thought that eating broccoli leaves was something shameful.

I stole a look at Mother and saw that she was biting her lips. For a couple of weeks afterward,

86

we had other vegetables for dinner. But in the end we went back to broccoli leaves.

Sometimes, when I looked at Mother spending so much time cooking, I felt very sorry for her. Her fine pianist's hands, which used to spend so much time over the keyboard, were now rough from washing vegetables and scaling fish.

If I could earn some money like Matthew and his brother, then Mother wouldn't have to work quite so hard trying to save money. Maybe I could deliver newspapers, too.

"Can I go with you on your paper round next time?" I asked him during school orchestra.

By now Matthew was getting used to my brand of English. "Paper route, you mean," he corrected. "Sure. But you have to get up early."

I could hardly believe it when he told me just how early. No wonder he was so sleepy. At five o'clock the next morning, I was struggling to put my clothes on in the darkness.

"Is it time to get up already?" mumbled Eldest Brother.

"No, it's early. I'm getting up because I'm going out with Matthew on his paper road."

"You're crazy," groaned Eldest Brother, burying his head under the covers again.

In Shanghai, we sometimes got up very early

on summer mornings because it was so hot that morning was the only comfortable time. But this wasn't summer. I shivered as I hurried to Matthew's house.

He was already waiting for me at the front door. "What kept you?" he asked. "We've got to hurry, since we have to fold the papers first."

My fingers were stiff with cold when I started to help Matthew fold the papers, but they soon warmed up. Then I watched Matthew throw papers at the houses along his route. "Do you want to try?" he asked after a while.

In the beginning I missed a few times, and some of the papers fell short or landed in bushes. I had to pick them up and throw all over again.

But my aim improved, and soon I was throwing the papers as accurately as Matthew. "It's just like throwing the ball from first base to the pitcher!" I exclaimed.

By the time we reached the end of Matthew's paper road — route — it was daylight, and I was starving.

Matthew looked at me gratefully. "I got through a lot sooner because you were helping. You're really good at throwing. I bet you can get a job delivering papers if you want."

When he told me how much he earned, I was

amazed. If I could get a job like this, it would really help our family. But would my parents let me?

I wasn't the only one in the family thinking about getting a job. Third Sister looked thoughtful at dinner that evening. She finally cleared her throat. "My shoes are wearing out. I saw some running shoes on sale at the store today. All the girls in school are wearing them."

Mother sighed. "You know we can't afford to buy you new shoes right now. You'll just have to have the old ones repaired."

"Maybe I can get a job and earn some money," Third Sister said brightly.

"A young girl like you, getting a job?" asked Mother, looking surprised. "What could you possibly do?"

"She can baby-sit," I said. I turned to Second Sister. "You can do it, too. Baby-sitting doesn't mean just sitting the baby in a chair. It means taking care of somebody's baby while the parents go out."

"You don't have to give me a lecture," snapped Second Sister. "I know what baby-sitting means. My friends in school told me about it."

I was surprised. It seems that Second Sister did not spend all her time brooding and longing for the old days in China. She had even made friends.

Second Sister turned to Mother. "Some of the girls earn a lot of money baby-sitting. If Third Sister and I do it every weekend, we can really help with the expenses. I think Mrs. Schultz might give me a job."

Mrs. Schultz was the mother of Father's youngest violin student, Peter. Second Sister often played with him until his mother came to pick him up. Once she was teaching him some Chinese children's games, and Mrs. Schultz was impressed.

Mother looked doubtful. "I can't imagine that parents will want to trust their babies to strange young girls." Then she added in a soft voice, "Especially Chinese girls."

The tone of Mother's voice was a shock. Had someone jeered at her because she was Chinese? She had never mentioned any unpleasant experiences before.

Then I thought of the two women in the

grocery store who had laughed at her for taking away big bags of broccoli greens. For some minutes we ate in uncomfortable silence.

Finally Father broke the silence. "No! I will not have any of my children earning money with little jobs outside the house! Young people should concentrate on what is important. You should not sacrifice your schoolwork and your music just to earn money for a pair of shoes."

"But . . ." Third Sister began.

Father was firm. "Music is more important than money."

We went back to eating dinner in silence. I was getting sleepy, and when I put down my rice bowl, I smothered a yawn.

Eldest Brother looked at me. "You got up too early this morning. What were you doing out of bed at five?"

This was not the time to tell everybody that I went out with Matthew because I was hoping to earn some money delivering newspapers. So I just mumbled something.

But that didn't stop everybody from staring at me. Father frowned. "If you have the energy to get up at five o'clock, you can surely spare some of it for your music! It's just a matter of channeling your energies into something worthwhile. You're a healthy, lively boy, Yingtao. Stop frittering yourself away on frivolous activities! Have you forgotten that the recital is coming up?"

Matthew and I saw less of each other, now that I had stopped playing baseball, and he had stopped coming over to our house for quartet practice. I was getting more and more worried about the recital.

"Will you still be able to play?" I asked Matthew, first thing on Monday.

"Yeah, sure, I try to get some practicing done when nobody's home," he replied quickly. But I couldn't tell if he was just saying that to stop me from worrying.

At my house, tempers were getting short. I was playing the second violin part all the time now, and the sound got on everyone's nerves.

One night, after some particularly hard measures, Eldest Brother threw his bow down. "We were doing so well for a while! What's wrong with you, Fourth Brother?"

Eldest Brother rarely lost his temper. We knew things were really getting serious.

Even Third Sister looked worried. She pulled

me aside when we finished playing. "The recital is only a couple of days away," she whispered. "What's happened to Matthew? Does this mean he won't be playing after all?" She looked sick at the prospect.

"Matthew will play," I said with more confidence than I felt.

Then on Friday, the day before the recital, my parents did something that would make it quite impossible for Matthew to play.

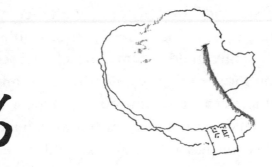

6

It happened at dinner.

"The quartet sounds just awful," Second Sister said gloomily. "It was much better when Matthew sat in with us. I think Fourth Brother always improved when his friend was around to encourage him."

"What's happened to Matthew?" Eldest Brother asked me. "Why hasn't he been coming lately? He didn't even show up for his lessons."

I stared down into my rice bowl. "His father got mad at him because he was spending too much time on music and not enough time on his baseball. So he won't let Matthew come to our house anymore."

I looked up and saw the Yang family in shock. Father's hand was suspended in air as he reached for a piece of fish. Mother's chopsticks were frozen halfway to her mouth. Eldest Brother's spoon was dripping soup on the table. Second Sister and Third Sister sat with their mouths opening and closing, like a pair of goldfish.

Our family could not imagine a father scolding his son for spending *too much* time on music.

Father recovered himself. "Maybe I should have a talk with the boy's father to convince him that his son has talent and should be encouraged."

"I have a better idea," said Mother. "Why don't we invite Matthew's family to the recital? Then they can see all the other young people happily playing their instruments. It might change their minds about music."

Across the table I met Third Sister's eyes, and I knew she was thinking the same thing I was. If the Conners came to the recital, Matthew would be sitting in the audience; he wouldn't be playing the second violin part.

"I don't think Mr. Conner would accept," I said carefully. "He hates the sound of the violin. He says the screeching hurts his ears."

"Then we'll have to convince him he's wrong," said Father.

Not with this recital, you won't, I thought to

myself. I made another effort. "Father, your students are having their first recital. They're going to be nervous, so they'll screech more than usual. Why not invite the Conners to the next recital?"

Father looked offended. "My students don't screech!"

Then Third Sister tried. "Maybe we can just invite Mr. and Mrs. Conner and let Matthew and his brother stay home and practice their baseball."

"Of course not!" said Mother. "Having Matthew here would help Yingtao's morale!"

"And besides," added Father, "Matthew has been helping Yingtao so much, it's only fair that he should come for the recital."

Third Sister and I knew that to argue any more would make our parents suspicious. We watched Mother go to the telephone to call up the Conners. I hoped desperately that they would be out or that they would refuse the invitation.

My hopes were dashed when Mother came back beaming. "I had to work pretty hard to persuade them, but they finally accepted." She turned to me. "Aren't you glad, Yingtao? I know you'll be doing your best, now that your friend will be here to hear you play."

That night, as Third Sister and I did the dishes, we tried to think what to do.

"Why don't you tell Father about your plan?" she whispered. "Tell him how much you want the recital to be a success, and that's why you want Matthew to play your part."

I thought of Father's sad face last week when I went to the baseball game with the Conners instead of practicing. "I can't do that," I said miserably. "He'll just think I'm not playing because I want to spend all my time on baseball."

"I guess you'll just have to play in the quartet," sighed Third Sister. "Anyway, it's more honest that way, and you'll feel better about it."

"It's more honest," I admitted, "but I won't feel better about it."

"Well, Matthew is smart," said Third Sister. "I'm sure he'll think of a way to play."

But maybe she was saying this just to calm my nerves, in case I had to play the next day.

Saturday came. I still hadn't heard from Matthew. I wanted to go over to his house to talk with him, but Father was keeping an eye on me, making sure I was staying home to practice.

Then I thought of calling Matthew up, but every time I went into the kitchen to call, someone was there. Second Sister was cutting up tea bags, or Mother was preparing the refreshments for the recital.

As the hour for the recital approached, I spent my time looking out the window, hoping for a sign from him. There was nothing.

The recital was being held in our living room, and it was to begin at two in the afternoon. Since Father had only six students, we could easily squeeze everybody in. The audience were mostly relatives — close relatives — of the young players, and we expected about twenty-five people.

Mother was going to serve orange soda to the young people and tea to the adults. She also planned to serve fortune cookies. We had actually never seen fortune cookies until we came to America. After Father got his first paycheck, he treated the family to a dinner in Chinatown. Although Mother was a good cook, we were glad to have a change. The food was Cantonese, which was a little different from the Shanghai food we had at home, but it was good and not totally strange.

The one strange item came at the end. When the waiter presented the bill, he also handed us a small plate with six funny-looking cookies. They were shaped like a small, round cake, folded in half, with the corners bent back.

"What are these?" asked Father.

"They are fortune cookies," said the waiter. "Each cookie has a piece of paper with your fortune on it." He showed us how to break the crisp cookie open and get at the tiny slip of paper with a message.

We excitedly broke open our cookies and read the messages. Mine said, "Listen carefully, and your inner voice will tell you what to do." Even my fortune cookie was telling me to listen carefully.

Everyone liked the fortune cookies very much. From that time on, Mother bought them for special celebrations. For the recital, she bought the largest package in the store.

"When the recital is finished, we'll really have something to celebrate," she said. She was smiling bravely as she spoke, but her voice trembled a little.

100

The only problem was how to get everyone seated. We finally borrowed enough chairs from our neighbors for the grown-ups. The kids in the audience would just have to sit on the floor.

Eldest Brother set up the screen in the living room. While he wasn't looking, I moved the screen a little so that it stood right in front of the door to the kitchen. This way Matthew could move to his place behind the screen without being seen.

If he came.

I could hardly swallow my lunch, I was so anxious about Matthew. Of course, the rest of the family thought I was just suffering from stage fright.

"You'll be all right if you just concentrate, Yingtao," Father said heartily.

"Don't finish your rice if you don't feel like it," said Mother. In our family — in any Chinese family — not finishing your bowl of rice is a terrible thing. So Mother was really trying to be kind.

"Once you get the first few measures right, the rest will come easily," said Eldest Brother. "I know you can do it."

Even Second Sister had a kind word to say.

"You have a good sense of rhythm, Fourth Brother. We all have confidence in you."

Could they be right? Maybe if I concentrated, maybe if I got the first few measures right . . . Maybe there was just a chance that I might not disgrace the Yang family after all.

For once, Third Sister was the only one who didn't say anything to cheer me up. Probably because she knew how hopeless it was.

After lunch Mother looked at the living room one last time and nodded. Then her eyes went to Second Sister's pictures of the Chinese scenes. "You've done a good job," she said softly.

We were still putting out the refreshments when the first of Father's students arrived with their parents. They were not only on time; they were early. I guess the parents were curious about how a Chinese family lived.

The kids probably just wanted to get it over with. Most of them didn't look happy about playing in front of people. I knew how they felt.

But stage fright was the least of my worries today. I hung around the backdoor, waiting and hoping for Matthew to arrive. When it was nearly two o'clock and most of the guests had arrived, there was still no sign of him. Slowly, reluctantly, I went to my room and got my violin out. Even the instrument seemed unwilling to leave its case.

"He's here!" It was Third Sister's voice. "He sneaked in through the backdoor without any-one seeing him!"

I spun around, and there, standing behind her, was Matthew.

For a moment we just stood there looking at each other. Neither of us could speak. I was too relieved to say anything, and Matthew too happy.

Then he grinned and made a thumbs-up sign. "I told my folks that I was coming down with something. I said it was better if I didn't go, in case the other kids caught it."

"Come on, we have to hurry down," whispered Third Sister. She was right. The others would be suspicious if we didn't show up soon.

I copied Matthew's thumbs-up sign, and hur-ried after Third Sister. According to our plan, Matthew was to wait in my room until it was time for the quartet, and then he would come downstairs, go through the kitchen, and get to his place behind the screen.

The program began right on time. Father had arranged the recital in order of age. His youngest student would play first, and then the next youngest, and so on. The last number was our quartet.

First on the program was Peter Schultz, who was five years old and the only boy among Father's students. Maybe he was too young to worry about being called a nerd, a wimp, or a sissy.

I was the same age as Peter when I got my first violin. But unlike me, Peter was not tone-deaf. His problem was that he couldn't count time. He didn't care if he played his notes too soon or too late, as long as he played them all. Mother accompanied Peter on the piano, and she had to scramble to stay with him.

At the end of the piece Peter bowed and beamed until his face almost split in two. We all clapped hard.

The rest of Father's students were girls. Four of them studied the violin and one of them the viola.

The string players in our school orchestra, the violinists, violists, and cellists, were almost all girls. But for some reason it was all right for boys to play wind instruments, like the trumpet and the clarinet. It couldn't have been easy for Matthew to keep on playing the violin, when the other boys teased him about it.

The girl who played next in the recital was terribly nervous. She was biting her lip as she played, and I found myself biting my lip, too. Once she had to stop in the middle of the piece because she had lost her place.

She looked ready to cry, but Father went over and talked softly to her for a minute. She started the piece over again, and this time she finished it. We clapped extra hard.

One of the older girls played a piece with a lot of fast notes. Some of the little kids in the audience said, "Ooh!"

At the end of the piece the girl bowed and quickly ran back to her parents. They hugged her, and I could hear them telling her how proud they were of her playing.

My parents had never told me they were proud of my playing. They never would, either.

I began to look over the other parents in the audience. Suddenly I recognized a couple sitting in the back row. It was Matthew's parents. When Mr. Conner caught my eye, he gave me a big wink. Eric wasn't with them, so he had managed to find an excuse to stay away.

The next three pieces seemed to pass very quickly. Much sooner than I expected, it was time for our quartet.

I jumped up and rushed over to help set up the music stands. As I was putting out the sheet music for the quartet, I noticed that the edge of one of Second Sister's paintings had come loose. There was a big gap, and I could see through it. If I could see through it, so could the audience.

"What's the matter?" Eldest Brother asked me. "Why are you taking so long?"

"The painting is coming loose here," I said. "I'll try to glue it back."

"Never mind!" hissed Second Sister. She seemed in a hurry to get the quartet over with. "Come on, let's get started."

"I won't be a minute," I muttered, and rushed into the kitchen.

Matthew was standing beside the refrigerator. "What's happened?"

"Haven't got time to explain," I gasped. "The glue! Where is the glue?"

Third Sister had used a tube of glue to put

up the paintings, and I didn't know where she had put it. Then I saw my bowl of leftover rice on the counter. I grabbed a bit of it and kneaded it together with my fingers until it became a sticky paste. Then I rushed back to the screen and quickly dabbed at the loose edge of the painting with my homemade paste. Third Sister soon saw what I was doing and helped me smooth the paper down.

"I didn't know that painting was so important to you," growled Second Sister. But she looked pleased.

The audience was getting restless, especially the children. We finally settled down in our seats. One of the mothers gave a "shush," and the children quieted. I heard a faint rustling behind the screen.

I glanced at Third Sister to see if she had also heard the rustle. She smiled at me, and her dimples flashed.

When I see her smile like that, I know she's thinking of some mischief. Now she was probably smiling because we were playing a trick on the audience.

Eldest Brother lifted his bow and began to play. Second Sister followed with her entrance, then Third Sister. As she played the deep notes of her cello, it was nearly time for my entrance. I lifted my bow. My fingers were sticky from the rice paste, but at least it gave me a better grip on the bow.

Eldest Brother gritted his teeth and Second Sister stiffened her shoulders as they prepared themselves for the sour notes they expected me to produce.

Then I drew my bow across the strings — or I pretended to. By now, I was really good at keeping my bow just a tiny bit above the strings. I was an expert at bow sync.

A ripple of notes came out as I moved my bow back and forth. Eldest Brother and Second Sister were so surprised that they both stopped playing for a moment. Only Third Sister's cello kept on going smoothly.

But Eldest Brother and Second Sister recovered quickly. They had both played in a lot of recitals back in China. Unexpected things often happen during a performance. They found their places again, and the quartet went ahead. To my great relief, Matthew was keeping up perfectly with the others.

It didn't take long for Eldest Brother to figure

out what was going on. From his seat, he could tell the second violin part wasn't coming from me. And soon he knew it was coming from behind the screen.

I saw Second Sister look at me. She had also figured out what was happening. She probably recognized Matthew's way of playing. But there was nothing she could do except continue to play, and play beautifully.

Everything was fine, until I took hold of the corner of the music to turn it over. The rice paste made my fingers stick to the paper. I broke out in a sweat as I tried to shake the paper loose.

Meanwhile the second violin part continued to issue smoothly from behind the screen. Did the audience notice that while I was struggling with the sheet music, my violin was playing by itself?

Maybe not. A lot of notes were flying around, and the audience couldn't always tell exactly which notes were coming from which player. Only the composer, Haydn, would know exactly, and he had been dead for almost two hundred years.

By the time I finally got my fingers free, my eyes were almost blinded by salty sweat. I wiped my brow and went back to swishing my bow back and forth.

I gave the audience a quick peek and saw that they all looked quite content. Mother smiled, and Father looked pleasantly surprised. They were proud of me.

My mouth filled with a bitter taste. My parents were proud of me for something I didn't do.

Suddenly I wished I had never thought of the trick. Third Sister was right. It would have been better for me to play the second violin part, even if I sounded terrible. At least that would have been honest.

But it was too late to change. Besides, Matthew was in this, too. The quartet kept on playing, and I went on moving my bow back and forth — silently.

The music became faster and louder as we got near the end. Eldest Brother had a short solo part with a dazzling swirl of notes that climbed higher and higher. After that, all four of us — all five of us? — played together, and we finished with a big, crashing chord.

The audience burst out clapping, even the little kids. I stole a look at Matthew's parents.

They were clapping as hard as everybody else.

It was time for the four of us to stand up and take a bow. Third Sister seemed to be having some trouble. We were crowded together, and she had to get her cello out of the way before she could bow properly.

Third Sister stepped back a little to give herself more room. She moved her cello to her left, and bumped hard against the screen.

Crash! In full view of the audience stood Matthew, with his violin still in his hands.

There was dead silence. I could see the audience trying to understand what was going on. Father and Mother were the first to suspect the truth. Their eyes went from me to Matthew and then back to me again. I swallowed hard, wanting to melt into a puddle and sink into the ground with shame.

Why was Matthew still standing there? He had promised to steal away as soon as the quartet was over! But I couldn't really blame him for staying. I think he wanted to hear the clapping. After all, he had earned it.

Father broke the silence. "So that's why the quartet sounded so different!" Shock was being replaced by anger on his face.

Mr. and Mrs. Conner just stood stunned, with their mouths open. Finally Mrs. Conner found her voice. "Matthew? What are you doing there? I thought you were sick!"

Matthew grinned sheepishly but didn't say anything.

Third Sister cleared her throat. "I'm glad you all liked the quartet," she said and smiled at the audience.

That was when I realized she had knocked

over the screen on purpose. She must have planned on doing it all along.

"Matthew isn't one of my father's regular students," she continued, "but we wanted to show you what a talented musician he is. So we played this little trick on you. We hope you enjoyed it."

She looked at me shyly, silently apologizing. I quickly smiled, letting her know that I wasn't angry at her.

There was a murmuring as the audience finally understood what had happened, that Matthew had been playing behind the screen. The kids loved the whole thing. They started cheering and clapping. After a while their parents joined in.

My parents were the only ones not cheering.

7

I was terrified of facing Father. He looked very angry, and I knew he would be having a stern talk with me at any moment.

But he didn't have a chance to talk to me at first. The recital turned out to a huge hit, much more successful than we had dared to hope. The parents crowded up to Father and congratulated him.

"To be frank with you, I didn't want to come to the recital," confessed the father of the girl who had been nervous. "These things can be a real pain in the . . . ow!"

His wife had kicked him. "We all had such a good time this afternoon!" she said. "After her other recitals, Alison would come home in tears. But today, she actually seems to be enjoying herself."

They looked around for Alison and found her with a group of other children reading their fortune cookie messages. We heard bursts of laughter.

The father of Peter Schultz, the little boy who had played first, felt the same way. "Your recital was as good as a show," he said. "It was a terrific idea to hide that boy behind the screen!"

Mrs. Schultz was talking to Second Sister. "I thought your quartet was beautiful! You must all practice an awful lot."

Second Sister glanced at me. "Yes, we practice long and hard, all five of us," she said darkly. Then she turned back to Peter's mother and smiled. "You're very kind."

A thoughtful look came over the face of Mrs. Schultz. "I wonder, do you do any baby-sitting? Peter seems to like you a lot. Do you think . . ."

Second Sister looked pleased. "I'll have to talk to my mother about it first."

When Second Sister told Mother what Mrs. Schultz had said, Mother looked surprised. "Are you sure you'd trust your son to a stranger?" She asked Mrs. Schultz. "A young girl like my daughter?"

"But your daughter isn't a stranger," protested Mrs. Schultz. "She's good with Peter.

Besides, I can tell she is a serious, responsible girl."

While Mother went off to talk to another parent, Mrs. Schultz and Second Sister began to talk about hours and rates.

Several of the parents came up to Father and said they knew people whose children would be interested in taking lessons. "You have such talented children!" said another parent. "You must be really proud."

Father looked more embarrassed than proud. When still another parent congratulated him on his talented children, he started to protest. "Actually, my youngest son isn't —"

Third Sister quickly interrupted. "Your daughter is pretty talented herself," she said to the parent.

I could see that Father was torn. He felt he should confess the shameful truth about Yang the Youngest and his terrible ear. But things were going so well — the parents were very pleased, and the children were all having a good time. Why spoil this nice party?

While the other guests were busy chatting, the Conners just stood there looking dazed. Nobody in the audience had been more amazed than his own parents when Matthew had been revealed behind the screen.

Third Sister brought some refreshments over to them and introduced herself. Mr. and Mrs. Conner still seemed to have trouble finding words.

Matthew finished putting away his violin and came to join his parents. "So it's true?" demanded Mr. Conner. "You were playing all those notes?"

Matthew grinned. "Not all of them, just some of them. In fact I played less than the others, because the second violin has the smallest part."

"But you kept up with the others," said Mr. Conner. There was awe in his voice. "They were all going a mile a minute, and you kept up!"

Mrs. Conner put her arm around Matthew. "I've never been so surprised in my life!"

Father, who was going around greeting all the parents, finally came to the Conners. Mr. Conner cleared his throat. "When your wife invited us, I was going to refuse. Didn't know you were planning this surprise for us."

Father shook Mr. Conner's hand. "You must be very proud of Matthew."

"We didn't know that the boy was any good,"

118

admitted Mr. Conner. "All we knew was that he spent a lot of time playing his violin."

"Matthew has a gift for music," Father said. "When someone has a gift for music, he will find a way to play, whether you want him to or not."

"You've certainly opened our eyes," said Mrs. Conner. "That must have been why Mary bumped into that screen. She did it on purpose, to let us know that it was Matthew who was playing."

Father looked bewildered. "Who's Mary?"

Mrs. Conner looked bewildered, too. She pointed to Third Sister, who was putting away orange soda bottles. "Isn't that Mary over there? Your daughter?"

"She means Third Sister," I told Father.

Mr. Conner grinned. "Kids can be real devils, can't they? I bet Mary and . . . er . . ."

"Yingtao," supplied Matthew.

"Yeah, Yingtao," said Mr. Conner. "I bet the two of them cooked up the scheme between them."

"Cooked up?" repeated Father faintly.

"I think what Mr. Conner means is that Third Sister and I planned everything together," I told Father.

But clearly Third Sister had her own ideas about how the recital should end.

I was glad she did it. I was glad that everybody now knew it was Matthew, not me, who had played the second violin part.

Mr. Conner's face became serious. "Do you think you could take Matthew as one of your students?" he asked Father.

Father looked uncomfortable. "I thought . . .

I thought my eldest son told me you are not working right now. He was giving Matthew some free lessons, and he would be glad to continue."

"We don't need charity," Mr. Conner said stiffly. "We'll find the money to pay you."

"Matthew earns some money himself," added Mrs. Conner. "He can help pay for his lessons."

"I'll be glad to pay for my lessons," Matthew said. "I mean it."

"He earns a lot of money delivering newspapers," I told Father. "He says I can do it, too, if you'll let me."

"You don't have time for a job," said Father. "You need to study and practice your violin."

"Aw, come on," said Mr. Conner. "Nobody needs to spend *all* his time studying and practicing. Besides, holding a job is good for a kid. Teaches him the value of money."

Father did not look convinced. "I have seen too many American youngsters earning money just to buy something trivial, like a pair of running shoes. Meanwhile their studies suffer."

"Not always," said Mr. Conner. "Take Matthew here. He delivers papers every morning, but he still gets decent grades in school." He added shyly, "And you could see he also did okay with his fiddle."

When Father didn't reply at first, Mr. Conner turned serious. "You just said yourself that when a kid has a gift for music, he'll play whether you want him to or not. Seems to me the opposite

122

is true, too. If he *doesn't* have a gift for music, making him practice won't do much good."

Father winced. Even Mr. Conner saw that his words were not very tactful. "Ouch! I shouldn't have said that. What I really mean is that people are all different. Now, Yangto . . ."

"Yingtao," corrected Matthew.

"Yeah, Yingtao. He's a great kid. And I really mean it."

"Yingtao is welcome at our house anytime," said Mrs. Conner. "He's a good influence on Matthew."

"You bet," said Mr. Conner. "I've never seen anyone pick up baseball so fast. If we're talking about gifts, he's got a real gift for baseball, your . . . er . . . Yingtao."

Father stared at Mr. and Mrs. Conner and then at me. "He's got a real gift? Yingtao?"

He had had a great number of surprises this afternoon, but this was the greatest surprise of all.

"That's right," said Mr. Conner. "You ought to come see him play sometime — then you'll see for yourself how talented he is."

When the door closed behind the Conner family, Father looked very thoughtful.

Mother and Third Sister were cleaning up,

while Eldest Brother and Second Sister went around returning chairs to our neighbors.

On her way back Second Sister drew me aside. "I'm proud of you, Fourth Brother."

All this praise was making me light-headed. First, it was the Conners, and now Second Sister, who had always been the most impatient with me.

"What do you mean?" I asked.

"You don't have to pretend," she said. "I know what you did. You gave up your place in the quartet so your friend could play. It was very generous of you, Fourth Brother."

"I just wanted the quartet to sound good," I muttered, embarrassed. "I didn't want to ruin the recital."

"That, too, was noble of you," she said. "You were sacrificing yourself for the good of the family."

Well, if she thought it had been a great sacrifice on my part, I wasn't going to try to change her mind.

That evening, as usual, we all went to practice. Eldest Brother practiced violin scales in our bedroom. Second Sister started a new viola piece in the living room.

Third Sister went into the bathroom and sat down on the toilet seat with her cello. She liked the way the sound bounced off the tiled walls. She also claimed that the carp in the bathtub splashed their tails to show they liked the music.

In the kitchen I sighed and took up my violin. I didn't try to tune it. What was the use?

But before I could tuck the violin under my chin, Father came in. "Yingtao, I want to talk to you."

My heart began to beat faster. It had come, at last, our talk. He was going to tell me I had disgraced the Yang family.

He sat down on a kitchen chair and made me sit facing him. "For years," he began, "your mother and I believed that you did not have the right attitude toward music, that you were simply not trying hard enough."

"I really do try hard," I protested desperately.

Father nodded. "After listening to the quartet this afternoon, I now believe you."

"But I didn't play this afternoon!"

"Precisely," said Father. "Day after day, I've had to listen to the four of you rehearsing, and always, the second violin part sounded . . ."

He stopped. At the thought of how the second

violin had sounded, a look of deep suffering came over his face, and the corners of his lips curled down.

"Then this afternoon," he continued, "I heard the quartet play as it had never played before. I was astonished. I never knew the second violin could sound like that."

"Because it wasn't me," I mumbled.

"Because it wasn't you," said Father. He took a deep breath. "I'm afraid you will never sound like that. You have to face the truth, Yingtao, even if it's very painful. You will never become a good violinist."

This was an important moment, and I tried to keep my face serious. But it was hard not to burst out laughing.

"I guess you can't make a silk ear out of a sow's purse," I said, quoting Third Sister.

Father looked puzzled. Maybe I had mixed up Third Sister's sentence.

"I'm glad you're taking this so well," said Father. "I'm proud of you."

8

In the days that followed, the family went out of their way to be nice to me. Actually, the nicest thing they did was to stop making me practice the violin.

I went around looking brave. Third Sister sometimes smiled at me as if we shared a secret. But I knew she wouldn't tell on me.

Matthew now came to our house to take lessons from Father. He insisted on paying, so Father charged him one dollar for each lesson.

I loaned Matthew my violin. He needed a better instrument than the school violin. The news about our recital got around, and when our orchestra conductor heard about it, he decided to give Matthew another audition. After the audition, the conductor moved Matthew to the front row, where the audience could hear him.

As for me, I told the conductor I wanted to give up the violin and play the triangle instead. He looked very relieved.

Matthew still plays quartets with my brother and sisters sometimes. On these days, Second Sister always asks me whether I mind being left out.

Of course I tell her I don't mind. But sometimes when I look at the four of them so wrapped up in the music, I remember a story I used to hear in China about a blind boy.

He was born blind, so he never knew what it was like to see colors. "Tell me again about the sunset," he would ask.

And people would try to tell him. They would describe the orange sky deepening into crimson and the edges of the rooftops lined with gold.

He would thank them politely, but they knew they had not been able to make him see how beautiful it was.

I felt like that blind boy as I listened to Matthew and the rest of the Yangs talking about a certain piece of music.

In the end, Father forgave me for not being able to play the violin. He even bought me my own baseball bat. But the best part was when Mr. Conner finally persuaded our family to attend a game our neighborhood team was playing.

It wasn't easy. "I have to practice," said Eldest Brother, shaking his head. "There's still one passage where I can't seem to get the fingering right."

"We don't know anything about baseball," complained Second Sister. "We'll be bored to death."

"I can explain what's happening," offered Mr. Conner.

Third Sister saw how wistful I was. "Fourth Brother listened patiently to music all these years, and he never complained about being bored. The least we can do is go to the game, just this once."

"All right, let's go," said Father. "I'm curious. I want to know what it is that makes Yingtao work so hard."

The game started badly. The other team was good, and they got two runs right in the first inning.

In the fourth inning, they got a man on first base, and one of their best hitters came up to bat. He could hit hard, so our outfielders got themselves ready for a line drive.

129

I was the shortstop, and I was close to the batter. From the way his eyes moved around, I guessed that he was going to try to bunt.

I was right. He swung his bat, and the ball bounced on the ground in front of me. I was already running for it. I scooped up the ball and threw it at the first baseman in a single unbroken movement. The batter was out, and the other side was retired.

In the cheers of the crowd, I thought I heard a girl's high, shrill voice. It was probably Third Sister. She could pick up American cheers faster than anybody.

Things began to get better. Our side made a run in the sixth inning. When I came up to bat in the seventh inning, we already had one man on first base and Matthew was on third.

I carefully wiped my hands on my pants. Something made me look up at the stands, where my family was sitting.

They were way up front, and Mr. Conner was leaning over, probably explaining the game to them. Eldest Brother looked bewildered, and Second Sister looked bored. Mother was frowning, but Third Sister was smiling. Father's face was expressionless.

I took a deep breath and faced the pitcher.

The first pitch was low and the second one way too high. I didn't even jerk my bat.

The third one seemed to be outside, but it curved a little at the last minute. By then it was too late to swing.

"Strike!" said the umpire. There was a murmuring from the spectators.

Another throw, this one definitely outside.

Was the pitcher going to walk me? The bases would be loaded then. But our side already had two men out, so the next hitter would have to make a hit.

Should I accept a walk, or should I try for a hit, even if the pitch was not a good one?

I glanced up at the stands, and my eyes met Father's. He nodded. Of course he understood nothing about baseball, but I knew what he wanted.

When the ball came, I swung at it with everything I had. It cracked against the bat and sent a shock up my arms like electricity.

I didn't wait to see where the ball went. I just threw the bat down, lowered my head, and ran like mad.

It wasn't a home run. Maybe I'll never live to hit a home run. But from the screams of the

crowd, I knew that Matthew had got home safely.

The roaring got louder. I slid into first base, picked myself up, and looked around. The boy who had been on first base had also made it home.

After that nothing could stop us. Our team got another run in the ninth, and we won the game. We filed off the field to the sound of cheers.

As I passed my family, I heard a tapping noise. I looked back and saw that Eldest Brother and Second Sister were smiling at me and tapping their bench with their pencils.

Suddenly I understood what they were doing. During a rehearsal, the string players sometimes want to tell a soloist or a guest conductor that they think he did well. They show their appreciation by lightly tapping their instruments with their bows.

Eric stared at Eldest Brother and Second Sister. "What are they doing that for?" he asked.

My throat was tight, and I couldn't answer. Matthew answered for me. "It's their way of telling Yingtao he did a good job."

"I'll say he did!" said Eric. "You could see that hitter was going to bunt, couldn't you, Yingtao? You've got a great eye!"

It made up for having a terrible ear.